Disney

STRANGE WORLD

W9-CBE-555

Meet the Clades

adapted by Natasha Bouchard

illustrated by the Disney Storybook Art Team

Random House 🏠 New York

Jaeger Clade is
a great explorer.
He is bold and strong.

Searcher Clade is

Jaeger's son.

He is quiet and gentle.

Jaeger craves adventure.
He wants to hike
over the mountain.
Searcher doesn't follow.
He wants to look
at plants.

Searcher is not
like his dad.
He does not want
to be an explorer.

Jaeger is angry.

He leaves

and never returns.

Many years later,
Searcher has a son.
His name is Ethan.
They are farmers.

Ethan is growing up.

He wants to have

his own life

and visit new places.

The leader of the city
needs Searcher's help.
Searcher must find out
what is hurting
the plants.

Searcher leaves his farm
for the mission.
He flies on an airship.

Ethan sneaks on board
the airship.
He wants to join
the mission.

Searcher gets lost
in a strange world.
He sees a hairy beast!

The beast is Jaeger!
Searcher is shocked
to see him alive.

Jaeger and Searcher fight scary creatures together.

They realize they are not so different.

Ethan explores
the strange land.
He sees amazing
creatures around him.

Ethan learns to fly
the airship with his mom.
He wants to be
an explorer.

Searcher thinks the
creatures hurt the plants.
Ethan will not
harm the creatures.

Ethan runs away.

Searcher follows him.

Then they see
a giant eye.

The land is alive!

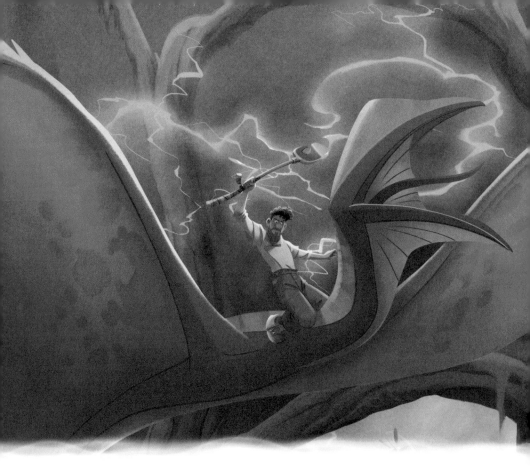

The creatures
are helping the land.
The plants are bad.
Searcher fights to
protect the creatures.

The plants hurt Searcher.
But he and his family
save the land.
The Clades are
happy to be together.

The Clades all like
different things.
But they love
their world—
and each other.

Dear Parents:

Congratulations! Your child is taking the first steps on an exciting journey. The destination? Independent reading!

STEP INTO READING® will help your child get there. The program offers five steps to reading success. Each step includes fun stories and colorful art or photographs. In addition to original fiction and books with favorite characters, there are Step into Reading Non-Fiction Readers, Phonics Readers and Boxed Sets, Sticker Readers, and Comic Readers—a complete literacy program with something to interest every child.

Learning to Read, Step by Step!

Ready to Read   Preschool–Kindergarten
• big type and easy words • rhyme and rhythm • picture clues
For children who know the alphabet and are eager to begin reading.

Reading with Help   Preschool–Grade 1
• basic vocabulary • short sentences • simple stories
For children who recognize familiar words and sound out new words with help.

Reading on Your Own   Grades 1–3
• engaging characters • easy-to-follow plots • popular topics
For children who are ready to read on their own.

Reading Paragraphs   Grades 2–3
• challenging vocabulary • short paragraphs • exciting stories
For newly independent readers who read simple sentences with confidence.

Ready for Chapters   Grades 2–4
• chapters • longer paragraphs • full-color art
For children who want to take the plunge into chapter books but still like colorful pictures.

STEP INTO READING® is designed to give every child a successful reading experience. The grade levels are only guides; children will progress through the steps at their own speed, developing confidence in their reading.

Remember, a lifetime love of reading starts with a single step!

Copyright © 2022 Disney Enterprises, Inc. All rights reserved. Published in the United States by Random House Children's Books, a division of Penguin Random House LLC, 1745 Broadway, New York, NY 10019, and in Canada by Penguin Random House Canada Limited, Toronto, in conjunction with Disney Enterprises, Inc.

Step into Reading, Random House, and the Random House colophon are registered trademarks of Penguin Random House LLC.

Visit us on the Web!
StepIntoReading.com
rhcbooks.com

Educators and librarians, for a variety of teaching tools, visit us at RHTeachersLibrarians.com

ISBN 978-0-7364-4330-2 (trade) — ISBN 978-0-7364-9030-6 (lib. bdg.)
ISBN 978-0-7364-4331-9 (ebook)

Printed in the United States of America
10 9 8 7 6 5 4 3 2 1